HANNA'S TREE
SEONG-MIN YOO

HANNA'S TREE
SEONG-MIN YOO

Tumbleweed Books
Tumble through the pages of our books

DAOwen Publications supports copyright. Copyright fuels creativity, encourages diverse voices, promotes free speach, and creates vibrant culture. Thank you for buying an authorized edition of this book and for complying with copyright laws by not reproducing, scanning, or distributing any part of it in any form without permission. You are supporting writers and allowing DAOwen Publications to continue to publish books for every reader.

Hanna's Tree / Seong-min Yoo
ISBN 978-1-928094-62-3

Artwork by Seong-min Yoo
Proofing by Scott MacKenzie
Edits and Layout by Douglas Owen

The artwork in this book was rendered in watercolour and the text is Kristen ITC

10 9 8 7 6 5 4 3 2 1

For my parents,

who are always a big piece of my heart,

now and forever.

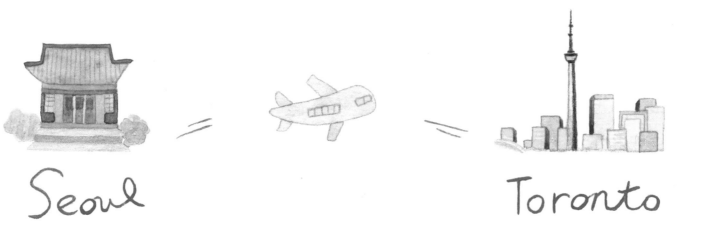

Seoul

Toronto

Hanna felt excited and scared at the same time.
Her family now lives in Toronto, having just
moved there from Korea only a few days ago.

When they landed, she could see
sparkly lights from the windows of
high-rise buildings as it was quite late.

Hanna felt a little restless because everything was unfamiliar to her. She was nervous because tomorrow would be her first day at school.

She could only understand a few words
of English that she had learned back in
Korea, and the rest of them sounded
like an alien language to her.
She thought, "How can
I understand them?"
"Can I use proper words?"
"Will I be able to make friends?"

Her worry grew and grew as many strange eyes
were on her at school the next day.

She felt like she was all by herself on a deserted island. Hanna heard kids asking questions.

"What's your name?"

"Where are you from?"

She became confused as to who was asking which questions. As kids popped up from everywhere, she answered them with only a few words. Then somebody said, "Can't you talk?"

Her face became red from embarrassment, and she didn't feel that this was the real her.

It was lunch, and Hanna sat in the corner by herself.
She opened her lunchbox to find some
kimbab and kimchee.

Some kids made faces as they passed by
and plugged their noses with their hands.
"Is that white stuff rice?"
"Do you eat rice every time?"
"I mean, all the time?" They giggled.
"What is that smelly thing?

This is pickled cabbage, and this is rice with vegetables rolled with dried seaweed, she said to the other kids in her head.

She felt a knot in her chest as she tried to keep eating, but she couldn't finish the rest of her meal.

Hanna sat in the swing outside after lunch until she heard the bell.

On the way home, she thought about the next day. Suddenly a big grey cloud formed over her head and it started to rain.

"How was school? You are soaked," her mom said, handing her some dry clothes, they felt so warm.

"It was okay, could you make just a sandwich for lunch tomorrow, please?"

She ran upstairs to her room and laid down on her bed, thinking, they really don't know me. How come they can say such mean things?

She looked out the window and didn't see anybody or have any friends to talk to.

A few days later, her mom bought a small, tiny tree that she carefully planted in front of her bedroom window. It was given to her as a gift.

Mom patted down the dirt to make sure the roots were buried nice and tight.

One day after school, as Hanna looked over the fence, she saw a girl living next door. Hanna was so happy that she found somebody whom she could possibly talk to.

The girl picked up something and swiftly disappeared. Out of curiosity, Hanna pushed a little gate and entered the garden, when suddenly everything vanished.

Hanna was startled as the girl approached her suddenly.

"My name is Nabi," she said. "Are you looking for this?"

Nabi handed a picture to her.

Later that afternoon, Hanna's family sat around the table. Hanna couldn't get rid of the mysterious girl from her head.

She pushed the chair away as soon as she finished dinner, and ran outside to see if Nabi was still there.

Sadly she wasn't.

She looked up at the sky and wondered what she would have been playing with her friends if she was still in Korea.

Her mind was full of thoughts about being back in her hometown.

Hanna baked some cookies with her mom one day, and she thought about the girl who handed her the pitcher. Mom opened the oven door, and a wonderful smell spread all over the house.

Hanna went outside to see if the little tree was doing well. Unfortunately, it was still small with no buds. She thought there might be something wrong with it, so she grabbed some more soil and added it to the tree.

She was looking over the fence when suddenly Nabi appeared. Nabi was feeding some birds.

"Do you want to try some cookies? I made them just now. Do you have a family? I haven't seen them," Hanna said.

"No, just myself."

"You can come over to play if you want," Hanna continued.

But Nabi went back to feeding
the birds without saying a word.

Hanna saw her mom on the porch.

"Who were you talking to?" she asked.

"My new friend," said Hanna.

That night Hanna saw Nabi carrying a basket, looking like she was going somewhere. Hanna followed her, but Nabi didn't notice.

Hanna saw Nabi go into a garden full of vines and trees. She heard a voice whisper, "Come in."

She climbed up a few steps feeling lightheaded. The branches of the tree seem like they were opening their arms, saying, "Please come in."

She wondered where Nabi was. "Come this way," she heard. "You don't need to worry about anything." Hanna looked around, surprised.

She could clearly hear Nabi's voice echoing through trees.

"Take your time, things will only get better, but you have to find the way by yourself," Nabi said.

The wind blew again. Hanna felt dizzy. She couldn't hear Nabi anymore. She felt lost.

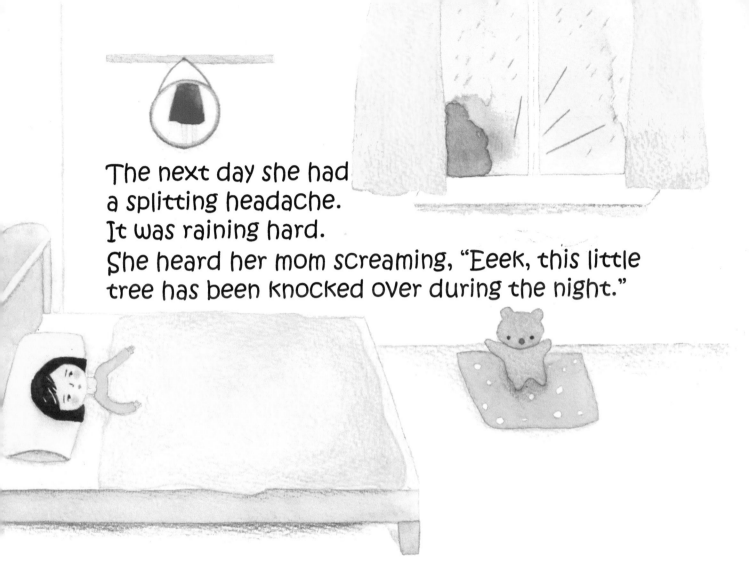

The next day she had
a splitting headache.
It was raining hard.
She heard her mom screaming, "Eeek, this little
tree has been knocked over during the night."

Hanna could vaguely hear the sound of a shovel.

As the sound of the digging got smaller and smaller, the familiar face at the corner of the bed got clearer. It was Nabi looking at her and holding little flowers of orange, yellow, and red.

"Cheer up, these are for you. I hope you feel better."

Hanna had never seen such beautiful flowers before.

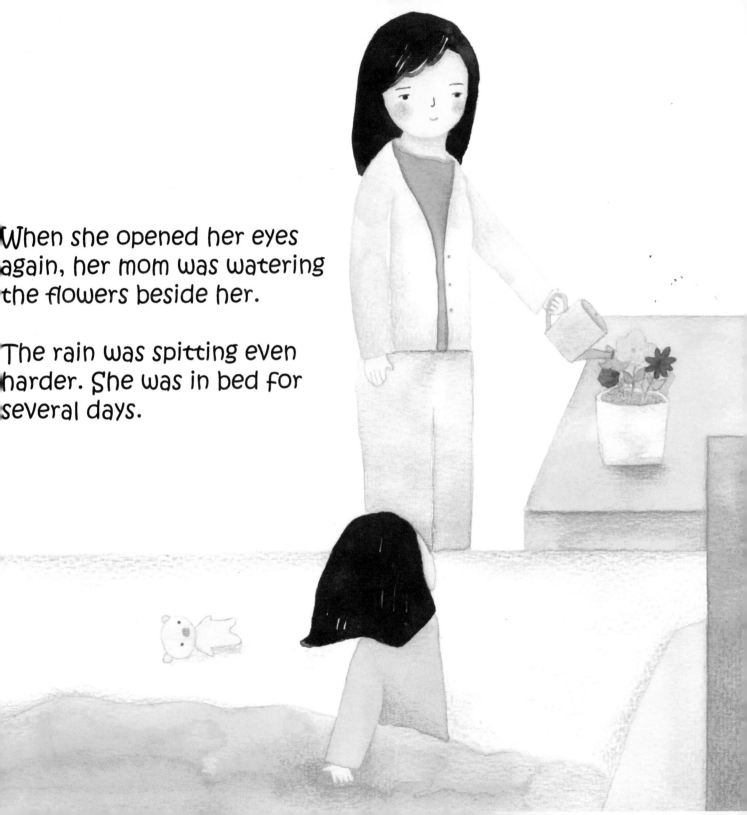

When she opened her eyes again, her mom was watering the flowers beside her.

The rain was spitting even harder. She was in bed for several days.

One day mom said, "You've been doing so well, I am sure you are going to get through this. We understand how much you still miss your friends and the things you loved to do back home."

Dad said, "But our feet are here now, and we are all in this together."

Hanna gave her parents a big tearful hug.

Busy days were spent at school. Hanna saw a few tiny buds shooting out from the tree. More days had passed, and Hanna walked home with some new friends she had made. Somedays, they entered the little gate through the garden and stayed there for hours playing together.

One beautiful summer night, Hanna noticed the tree's blossoms through the window. She suddenly realized the tree that had trouble growing, now had so many beautiful flowers. She ran downstairs to get a better look.

She saw Nabi sitting in the tree and smiling at her. She rubbed her eyes, Nabi looked a little different. But the tree was shining so brightly, she couldn't see her properly. However, she heard what she said very clearly.

"Don't lose yourself. Always know that you are stronger than you think."

As Nabi disappeared into the tree, Hanna saw the tree give her the most genuinely warm smile. It made her heart so full.

Other works by Seong-min Yoo

MEMORIES OF KOREA

SEONG MIN YOO

BEAVER'S CRAZY SLEEPOVER

Seong-min Yoo

BEAR'S
DANCING SHOES

SEONG-MIN YOO

CPSIA information can be obtained
at www.ICGtesting.com
Printed in the USA
LVHW071942280423
745593LV00015B/103

* 9 7 8 1 9 2 8 0 9 4 6 2 3 *